Copyright © 2022 by Kefentse Booth

All rights reserved. No part of this book or any portion thereof may not be reproduced or used in any manner whatsoever without the express written permission of the publisher except for the use of brief quotations in a book review.

Printed in the United States of America

ISBN 978-0-9977409-4-3 (Hardcover)

ISBN 978-0-9977409-5-0 (Paperback)

Published by Street Light Dreams, LLC, Detroit, MI

www.StreetLightDreams.com

Kisses Don't Last Forever.

Table of Contents

To Whom It Does Concern, ... VII

Broken Love 1
    Unrequited Love 2
    Negative Connotations 3
    I'm Not Happy 4
    Skeptical 6
    Boxcar Blues 8
    Weighted Love Affair. 10
    Unpacked. 12
    Lost and Turned Out 13
    Barbed Wire 14
    I Lay My Burden 15
    Woman in the Window 17
    After All the Love We Made. 18
    We lost! 20
    Caged Bird 21
    Broken. 23
    Star-crossed 24
    Celebration of Freedom. 26

Lost Loves Residue 28
    Scars 29
    Kisses Don't Last Forever 30

Soft fibers touch with igniting receptors. 30

I Regret 32

Truth Be Told 35

Junk Mail 37

Smile. 38

The Dress 41

Wedded Substitutes 43

Kept Place for Him 45

Season of… 47

Visions. 50

Love Re-Enters. 51

Hummingbird 52

Dear Father Time 54

Idle Ideation 56

I Apologize 58

Yesterday 60

Soul Mates 62

A Brilliant Tragedy 63

Time and Space 65

Dreamscape 66

Weathered Tone. 68

A Touch of Tomorrow 70

Message to a Difficult Person 72

The Photograph. 74

Loves Flames Rekindled 76
    The Freedom of Love. 77
    Simply Beautiful. 79
    A Flickering Amber. 81
    Last Time 83
    Bottle Rockets and Boat Anchors 84
    Love Note 87
    7 Days Ago 88
    Sleepovers 90
    Brown Eyes 92
    Speak To Me 93
    Submissive 94
    Nature At Its Best 95

Love Next Steps 96
    Frozen Moment. 97
    Angel Number. 98
    Admiration 100
    Are You Complicated to Love? 102
    Reassurance 104
    Dancing Sunshine 105
    Dreams and Nightmares 107
    Build Me Up 109

Pieces of Love 111
    Marvelous Curves. 112

Unimpressed.	113
Distanced Traveled	115
Heart to Heart	118
Pen Pals	120
Mercury Retrograde	122
To Whom It Does Concerns,	124

To Whom It Does Concern,

I fell in love with you during changing seasons and casual conversations. I purged my wants with the smiles you casted my way. I needed your attention to detail like answers to vital questions. If you had a moment, I dreamt about me being everything inside it. Coded language with two fluent hearts. I wanted you to have mine. To have and hold. To cherish and learn. Upon my chest to sleep as your lungs shared euphoric air. You gave me life when my world was fleeting. You colored outside the lines I knew and painted imagery of marvelous hues.

I fell in love during the day and night. Between morning and afternoon. You were my meaning of time and time has always made time for us. Witching hour kisses turned into great morning memories. Undeniable slow dancing to our connected rhythm and blues. You were music to my tone-deaf ears. Subtle strings with joy in a voice unlocking my soul. You fit physically, mentally, and spiritually. We tied our soul in a knot stronger than our reality knew.

I was in love with love and allowed love to drive away. Out my eyesight and miles of distance we suffered. While creeping through the years as more than friends I found substitutes. Mere fragments, pieces of you. Low hanging fruit tasteless and unfulfilling to my needs. I needed to tell you something. Anything more than what I was saying. More than breathing shells with blocked emotions we withered what we had. Cast it into an abyss we knew all so well. Out of sight and out of mind we moved on. Yet, my heart stayed with you, and I am unable to give something to someone else when the possession is forever yours.

I should've told you how I felt. Told you that I let you grow and not let you go. I should've been there, forged a bond in real time outside of closed doors and your watered garden. I should've protected you when you needed me to shield you. I should have chosen you. Showed you that you were enough, and I was the lacking entity that hindered our moment. You were finding yourself and I lost my reason. My reason to churn my potential energy into the power that willed our wants. Your dreams; of us.

I wanted what you wanted. I saw the future and was scared of my then present. At that moment, I should have come to you. Laid in your lap and let you deliver the evils from my soul. I should have invested more than the dejected corpse you learned to love. Just as you learned to love me, you learned to love without me. On lips that weren't mine you kissed forever in the atmosphere. Within my regrets I watched from the shadows.

I unbuckled the safety restraints and exited off our carousel. Periodically I would peek into your life, roam my thoughts within your still renderings and drift on a memory. It had been years since we'd last seen one another, but when we did it was magic. Invigorating hugs with a deep inhale of your custom fragrance. Laughter and chiseled moments like old times were present. I never wanted to let go but we were mandated. Those days I still failed to tell you my thoughts, so I buried them with content to never speak of them again.

Who ever knew souls speak when mouths are muted? I felt you through distance and space. We were still breathing in universes that connect us forever. You've loved before. I've loved before. But have you ever stopped loving me to allow yourself to fully love the person you are with? Have you let go to never latch back on? Would you rescue me if you knew you knew I needed you? I would for you. Free-falling and alone, I'll wrap you in my comfort. Kiss your forehead and move a mountain. Be your anomaly like tornados in winter. Hold you tight and not sleep through the night. Cherish the moment and marvel at the way we spoon daylight in and out of our days. If only it was that simple.

Letters are direct dialect without interruptions. Well, this is my heart catching up to my soul. My coded message written in our language hidden amongst the stars. Joyous picture reels of past endeavors perusing into my present. Time. Space. Communication. I'll always love you.

Kisses don't last forever but a love like ours definitely does.

Sincerely,

Your Twin Flame

Broken Love

Unrequited Love

Do you feel the air growing calm around us?

No breeze from the cracked windows.

No rotation from the fans.

We're stagnate!

At a loss for words as we search for clarity.

Our magic is gone.

Missing emotions giving way to dormant reactions.

We twist and turn but crash and burn.

Our intimate activities lack participation awards.

We were great once before.

Now our love language only hears and speaks our evils.

Negative Connotations

Your negative vibes pour through.

Your inability to corral your emotions spew from your lips.

You blame everyone except yourself.

You stare in the mirror during pitch black settings.

Who you want to be will never happen?

Where you want to go will never see you.

When it's all said and done, you'll be you!

A lonely soul that never got the chance to understand yourself.

A vessel with limited love and loved on by default.

So, carry on Joy stealer!

Transfer your lot to anyone willing to absorb.

Give all your hate along with all your minuscule maneuvers.

I'll give you two birds that flock to your soul.

I'm Not Happy

I'm not happy.

Life moves and I'm stagnate.

Stagnate with living to my full potential.

Potential to be greater than my current.

Currently I'm loving.

Loving a vessel that reaps all the benefits.

Benefits that project a deceitful story.

A story of miscommunication and fairytales.

Fairytales of happily ever after.

Miscommunication of wants.

Wants that I needed to manifest.

Manifest into my everything.

Everything isn't available.

Isn't available to fulfill my dreams.

Dreams that I held through the years.

Years that seem to have taken a toll on me.

On me!

My happiness is on me.

Me first, anyone next.

Next time, I'll be wiser.

Wiser than the me I plan to kill.

Kill by closing doors and walking feet.

Feet that didn't move your way.

Way back when I was in love.

In love with so much about you.

So much in love with your potential.

Potential that I now know you maxed out.

Out of time and space we stare.

Stare into the eyes of what never will be.

Be it as it may, I had a role in this.

This will hurt you.

You have given me years of your life.

Life that I'm grateful to be a part of.

Of all the things I can tell you, I say this.

This isn't happiness.

Happiness doesn't chokehold a soul.

Doesn't take breath without giving.

Doesn't move without unison.

Doesn't cause more frowns than smiles.

Doesn't break a heart and not repair.

I'm not repairable.

Not available to allow you to try.

Not present spiritually. I'll try to keep this brief.

I'm Not Happy!

Skeptical

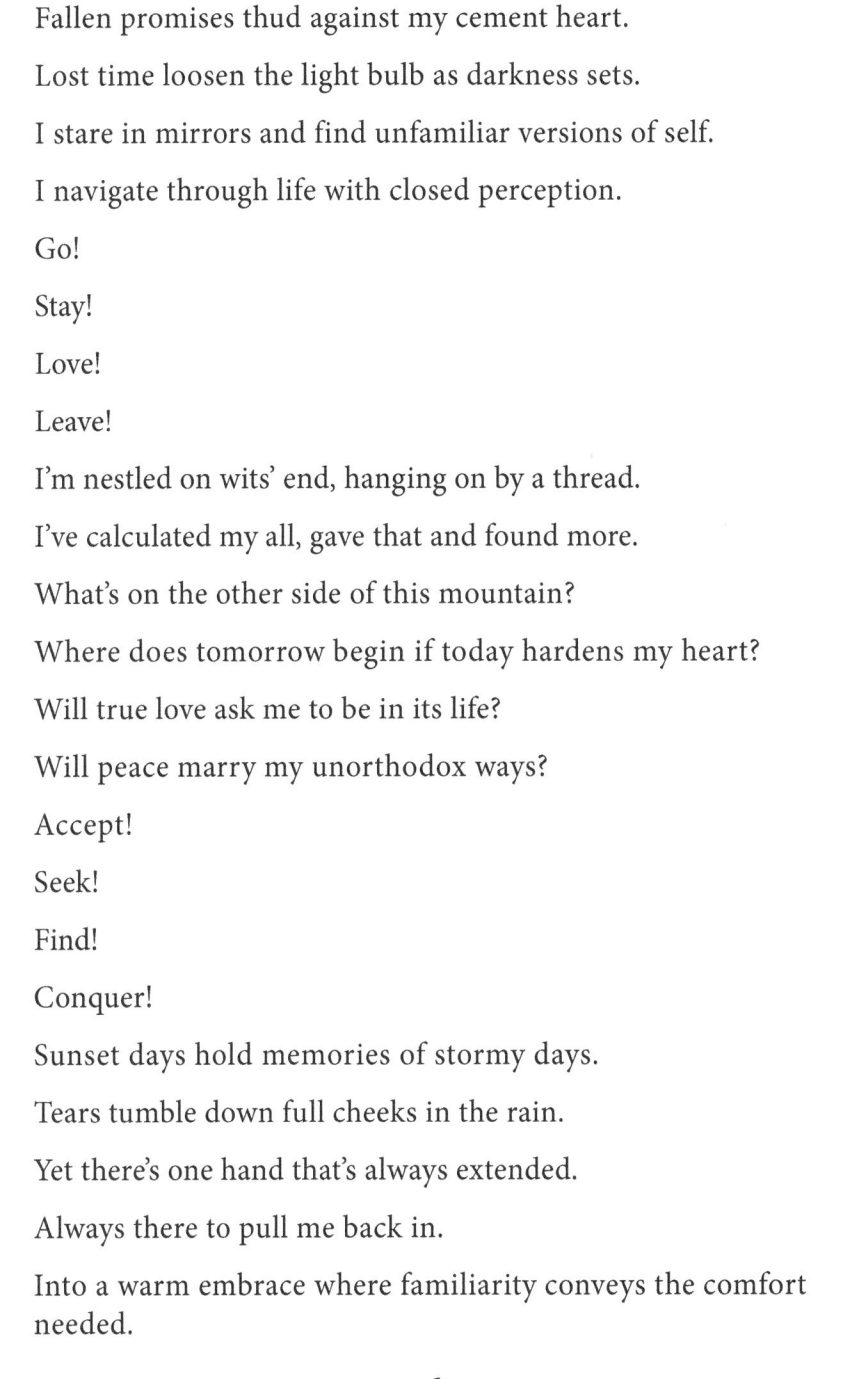

Fallen promises thud against my cement heart.

Lost time loosen the light bulb as darkness sets.

I stare in mirrors and find unfamiliar versions of self.

I navigate through life with closed perception.

Go!

Stay!

Love!

Leave!

I'm nestled on wits' end, hanging on by a thread.

I've calculated my all, gave that and found more.

What's on the other side of this mountain?

Where does tomorrow begin if today hardens my heart?

Will true love ask me to be in its life?

Will peace marry my unorthodox ways?

Accept!

Seek!

Find!

Conquer!

Sunset days hold memories of stormy days.

Tears tumble down full cheeks in the rain.

Yet there's one hand that's always extended.

Always there to pull me back in.

Into a warm embrace where familiarity conveys the comfort needed.

Umbrella held high to shield me while we're present.

One wink warms the heart and changes the climate.

Is this really life?

Happiness wrapped in the form of forever.

I'll let them take the first steps as I inch closer.

I need to know I have all of them.

Maybe we'll finally get our time to grow together.

Till then I'll hold fast to my thoughts and memories.

Unconvinced that this world would grant me a prayer of that magnitude.

Boxcar Blues

I called you didn't answer
I wrote you didn't respond
I whispered in the winds
I double clicked your pictures
I gave you my heart
Still you didn't communicate

I wondered inside our corridor
Housed inside my mind
I search within our meeting places
My soul cried as you hide and I seek

I'm chasing and your running
Under shooting our right now
Over shooting my thoughts

I'm thinking with bad intentions
Harbored nightmares of future lost
Realistic renderings of time wasted
Death to connecting with love again

I carry my heart upon stick and handkerchief
I jump boxcar to boxcar for comfort

I'm traveling inside a world without meaning
I rest on hardened lessons that life has taught.

Inside dreams I reach for you
Your smile! It still provides comfort
Your touch! It feels so real
Your voice. It lullabies my frame to rest.

If only I could get to you
Outside dreams
Inside reality
If only I could give you me

Would you accept me
Cherish the future
Forgive the past
Make anew in the present

My mind is laboring
My heart is overworking
Weary is this corpse
That houses a soul with you as its true love.

I'll call again soon, please answer!

Weighted Love Affair

She had her world plus the universe

hunkering down as an anchored weight.

Ramped thoughts running marathons around tracks of emotions.

Stoic expressions within framed reels concrete her smile.

The war of worlds raged on inside her home.

Never did her life become whispers in the streets.

Simplicity with complex movement.

The epitome of style and grace.

A sheik chronograph calculated with precise accuracy.

Then there was the man in her shadows.

Hidden in the backdrop with something different.

He vaulted the transgressions.

Caressed her idle time with passages that communicated with her soul.

Yet he was inevitably a ghost!

Visible to her.

Dormant to others.

And obsolete if anyone pried.

They were realizing they were beautiful music.

Luxury fabric cut from the same cloth.

They were simultaneous heartbeats miles away.

Simultaneous currents of energy wondering if they would fully collide.

He wanted to release her weight.

Provide her time to heal the bruises.

But his shadow danced upon a thin line of disrespect.

Maybe the dark corridor of her memories is where he needed to live.

Forever in their moment, but never in her present.

He now became additional weight from their wants to be together.

Unpacked

He was there to carry her suitcase.

Attentive and understanding,

he stayed as she unzipped to expose.

All her feelings and thoughts release.

She wants to cry at the confusion,

but he's right there.

Cemented in position to sort through the mess.

He owns his mistakes that caused her inverted walls.

One by one they sift through as emotions cruise through the air.

For her he'll pluck stars out the sky and jar them for a night light.

Lay next to her and shield away any nightmares.

It will take some time to unpack everything, and he is willing to stay.

Yet some things are meant for her eyes only, so he exits till she tells him she's ready.

When he enters back, she's free.

He's free.

Unpacked and unboxed.

Life looks brighter as the jarred stars light up their future.

Lost and Turned Out

Dark corridors of yesteryear.

Fermented stench within narrowing fear.

Closing walls incubates my cries.

Hidden agendas inside my lies.

I have arrived!

Settled into an abyss that loses my soul.

Turned outside nestled inside a hole.

Sunshine of today hurts my glance.

Smoke screams in my lungs as my demon's dance.

Eyelids heavy.

My mind soaring past earth.

Space!

Universe!

Nebulas!

High off hurt!

Barbed Wire

I built these walls from brokenness and hurt.

Labored my love as the tears mortared the brick.

Stone after stone, you refused to accept my internal working.

Brick after brick I secured a perimeter.

When you got crafty, I built a moat.

When you tried to scale the walls, I barbed wired you out.

In the center of my castle, I soak.

Deep sorrows with a desire to love.

You yell my name for attention.

I cover my ears for sanity.

You're too blind to see all of me.

I'm too tired to fight you anymore.

Yet, there's that one that knows how to get in.

Forever using their key at just the right time.

No judgement or misconstrued interpretations.

They get me.

While you bang your head in search of ways to understand.

I comfortingly allow the arms of another to secure me.

Sealing our connection with a gentle touch of a forehead kiss.

I Lay My Burden

Raised voice with hard questions.
Questions that were directed at me but not mine.
Immediate want to have my words tell her something.
Yet, I knew better.
Knew her a little not to say anything.
To try and mute the emotion.
Delay her want for an answer, only to vent out her issues.
And vent she did.
Words formed sentences that collided with her truths.

She was hurting!

Depleted by the actions of another man.
A man that promised the world and took her land from her.
Oh, how he neglected to submit to her.
Disregarded her needs and did whatever he wanted.
That man took beauty and caged her growth.
Anxiety and disbelief seeping from her pores.
I never seen her this fragile.
And here I stand!
In the gap for a friend that I love.
In a space that she carved out for me.
Behind her fortress walls standing in direct line of fire.
His line of fire but my presence.

Why am I here?

Because her pain urgently called my soul.

Her tears needed my thumb to gently wipe them away.

For my eyes to stare in her face.

I was cemented within her life.

Equipped to weather this storm with her.

If her foundation cracks, reconstruct her structure with love.

Mend her heart with words.

Touch her with affection.

Kiss her with love.

Hold her with protection.

Simply be there!

Be there to unmask her.

I crumble her walls.

I free up time to create moments.

I use the tears he caused as glue to piece her together.

His vengeance to sculpt her beauty.

His departure to walk through our once closed door.

Yet, before I cross the threshold,

we take out his baggage he caused.

Wiping his feces from our shoes.

Stomping upon a mat at his once home that read "Welcome!"

Woman in the Window

Open blinds to my closed heart.

Bystanders walk past then disappear.

Here one minute, gone the next.

Love has fled and my heart is fleeting.

Seated fetal position with weary looks.

Draped in his shirt I smell his scent.

Love once filled my lungs.

Now my heart pumps with only an ounce of blood.

My old self is missing!

Fixed eyes on solemn faces.

So much life outside my window.

Yet our love died inside the home I sit.

I watched as it drove off.

Vulnerable and exposed.

Disengaged and alone.

My windowpane tells two times.

Morning sun and night's darkness.

Everything else doesn't matter.

After All the Love We Made

Was it you and me?

Or was it you and the skeletons in the closets that hung next to my clothes?

I walked down hallways of our house with locked doors.

Hidden corpses with last breaths full of moans.

I was your key.

A key unable to turn your latch to release all of you.

All the compartments that you buried.

Buried next to our relationship.

A relationship that was supposed to be built on love.

Obviously built on a cracked foundation.

The crack in my heart that spread as I unmasked who you really are.

My clear view stares into the face of a lie.

You never killed yourself to make a new life with me.

You never pressed forward to never look back.

Smooth, subtle words with a hint of deceit.

I should've smelled it on your breath.

Should've felt the third party jumping in our bed.

Should've had an in-depth conversation with my intuition.

Should've seen her marking territory with scratches on your back.

I must've missed the lipstick on your collar.

Our inability to truly connect.

You're the unenjoyable ticking of a clock that's lost its minute hand.

Absent calendar pages turning as sunup feels like death, and sunset like freedom.

I laid next to nothingness for too long.

I believed in an abyss of loveless,

squandered moments wading in the waters of tears.

You were the closed door in a home of mortar and bricks.

Bricks that should've been thrown like stones in a glass house.

The way that I love you has me questioning myself.

The way I love you has me ready to pay my lawyer up.

The way I love you will have me in the backseat of a cop car.

Ready to be booked as they figure out the charges.

I would talk to someone, but I only confide in you.

And since I heard those corpses moan your name, I feel like snatching your soul.

The heart they think they have belongs to me.

We lost!

Somehow, we both lost the ability to insert actions.

We played it safe, and safety kept us close.

Safety created a smokescreen.

Safety eliminated touch.

And touch is what we needed.

Touch through words.

Touch through kisses.

Touch through time.

Touch from space.

Touch through the fibers of our existence.

We lost touch!

Caged Bird

It's a confusing feeling that engulfs me.

Any time we are off I wade in the water and search for answers.

We're not clicking.

Got it!

Make the next move your best move, I say to myself.

Deep breaths and leapfrog thoughts ricochet.

Her mood is the most important thing to me at this moment.

Her smile is the next thing I'm searching to find.

A way into a heart I'm trying to win is last.

Ultimate goal is to not become "the" problem.

She stops her day for me.

Allows me entrance and I try to access her.

She's closed off.

I'm locked out.

My master key works but the deadbolt is stuck.

I'm working for common ground.

Maybe space is her need.

But why did she allow me entrance?

Allowed me her time.

Her space.

A sample size of her day.

Why am I overthinking.

She's free to fly alone.

Free to saturate in her alone time.

I'm only a voice.

A voice that doesn't have the code for conversation today.

Cordial and sweet, I fold my hand.

I'll love her from a distance.

Await her communication when she's ready.

Check on her via scribe.

And long for her in the interim.

Until I unlock my cage and fly freely in open skies,

I refuse to be anything remotely resembling the cage that once locked away her joyful songs.

Broken

Broken communication led to shattered futures.
Stable hearts with irregular paths.
Two flames flicker on windowsills miles apart.
Conversation with constellations above for answers.
God must be tired of me asking for answers to the same questions.

If only I could feel their touch.
Bask in their aura.
Lose myself in their arms.
Sleep with their goodness.

Don't dwell on the past, let it be and move on.
Yet, my past is present holding a future that I long.
Our brokenness connects to tell a story.
Our story!
Our love!

I listen to the sweet tones of Love's voice.
That memory lives on behind closed eyelids.
That voice that never told my soul "Goodbye."
That voice that had my soul at "Hello."

Star-crossed

I don't know how she fell in love with me.

The mystery within the thought softens my core.

In a universe full of stars, she was mine.

The sun to my warmth.

The light to my days.

My twinkle during night.

The ray of light during clouded moments.

Her heart talked for her.

She loved with affection.

She caressed with her touch.

More than her attributes she keyed my lock.

She turned, then opened.

Climbing into my soul she closed the door.

She invaded my space.

Caused time to wait on us.

Many days she just laid there.

My right arm as her pillow.

My lips on the top of her hair.

Left arm wrapped around her torso.

I inhaled her scent, feeling a smile grace her face.

When I had her I should've asked.

"Why do you love me?"

Whatever the answer would've been in that moment

would've been perfect.

Because in moments I didn't speak.

I didn't release my feelings for her heart to hold.

To nurture and feel wanted.

I didn't give her a foundation to feel like enough.

I built the roads from the tears that traveled her cheek for me.

Bricked the wall that stood as she enclosed herself in.

I provided friendship but not love.

I gave her time.

Yet, only in the pasts present and not the forever future.

My sun was my star.

And my star still kisses my soul with her warmth.

Celebration of Freedom

Lethargic and unapologetic.

Closed off and nestled.

The bed swallows her want to leave.

Thoughts of color combinations play dress up.

A smirk graces her face.

If she pairs those shoes with that dress.

That blouse with those pants.

Earrings and bracelets.

Handbag or clutch?

Whatever it is, the night is hers.

Her time is now.

New bounce in her walk.

She sings while she dresses.

Stares into a mirror and loves her image.

No curfew to keep.

No chains holding her captive.

Someone is going to see her,

and that someone is everyone.

Pour a glass of wine.

Mix a drink of choice.

Play her favorite song.

Dance like the floor is hers.

Freedom like wings flow from her back.

Free like soaring alone, seeing heights unknown.

Glasses in the air.

Hips moving to her own beat.

It's a celebration of life.

Toast to the new her!

Lost Loves Residue

Scars

Surgical knives apply pressure.

Precious skin detaches.

Oxygen changes color.

Blue blood runs red.

Surgery repairs deep inside.

Gauze clean up my mess.

Scalpel cut and stitches sew.

Scars leave surface marks.

Some major.

Some minor.

Healing comes with time.

Emotions have good and bad days.

Spiritual warfare versus internal healing.

Forever memories married to the past.

Kisses Don't Last Forever

Soft fibers touch with igniting receptors.

Closed eyes with colliding bumper car thoughts.

Warm embraces that heat our core.
My butterflies do aerial somersaults.

Savory scent serenades my senses.
Vibrant voice sings lullabies.

Love landing on and off our lips.
Life living within moments.

Stones unturned exposing our faults
We were everything to everyone.
A storied love chronicle read aloud.
Mountaintop manifestos carved in glaciers.
Created constellations etched in heavens sky.
The language of love looming for lifetimes.
Breezing winds of hope as bystanders glazed.
An infinite amount of sand cradled within our hourglass.
A face full of serenity sun setting with marvelous hues.
Midnight hallucinations has me reaching.
Searching for anything to still grab hold too.

Our rose petals wilt.

Time gave up on us.

Fibers of lips now kiss with lackluster shine.

We exit with streaming tears.

Goodbye to yesteryear.

Sunshine on windowpanes briefly resurrects a smile.

Moonlit stares have me tracing our stars.

Deep breaths with eyes closed reminisces on love.

Yet, yesterday doesn't last forever.

Tomorrow wasn't our promise.

Just intertwined souls with a loose knot.

Passion and pleasure sealed with a kiss.

A kiss that didn't last forever.

I Regret

I regret being your friend.

I mean,

I regret being that friend.

That friend that fell in love with

The love of my lifetime.

The love within adjacent universes.

The unbreakable love.

The connection.

Connection to your essence.

Your chemical makeup.

Your universal key to all your doors.

I gained your trust.

Your body.

Your mind.

Your soul.

Our souls married without rings.

Our lives intercepted without force.

Comfort and familiarity at first sight.

Protection and honesty through eons.

Only time plays ticking clocks

That tocks at our lock.

Holding space between our touch.

That touch of atoms igniting.

Receptors moving muscles in our faces.

Adornment of right now.

Admiration of the past.

Affirmation of a future.

With seasons flowers at full bloom.

Popping colors like fireworks in summers sky.

I regret the regret that collided with my comfort.

The one that changed my cognitive patterns.

That altered my confidence.

To fight for love.

Inside reality's peripheral.

That eliminated hope.

To fight for forever.

Inside my present arrogance

that love always revolved around you!

Like roulette Russian rules I'll gamble.

On life.

This life.

Could be life.

Would be life.

Only if friendship forge a new love affair

That cascade on waves like runners.

Catching a breeze through the follicles of many days

Like the strands of hair counted.

Loving you is the greatest reflection of myself.

Until mirrors house my lips to forehead

I'll regret.

I'll regret myself for not chasing.

For not seeking and finding.

For not communicating with words.

For not letting my soul be heard.

I regret my regret to regretfully tell you

My biggest regret is the lack of us in this world that we both live in separately.

Truth Be Told

I was scared to love you.

Scared to release complexity for simplicity.

Scared to allow you to stay!

Stay past the night.

Stay past daybreak.

Scared to allow you to stay forever!

I crushed on you.

I stared at you and soaked in your aura.

Beauty smiling with sun kissed skin.

Personality gushing with each movement.

You commanded attention.

My attention.

I was in fear of you.

Somehow you eased my pain.

Gave me new reason to find what I'd lost.

That thing was love!

I fell in love with you!

Multiple times.

Multiple ways.

Commanding my attention and time.

I gave you me!

Left doors unlocked.

You entered and laid.

We melted as one.

I held you nightly like protection.

Made you as comfortable as I could, you slept in peace.

I gave all I could but not enough.

We parted ways without closure.

I was scared to let you leave.

Yet, I left.

Scared to misuse you.

Yet, I was taught lessons.

That love hurts.

That kisses don't last forever.

I was scared to love you back,

Because loving you would hurt if we departed.

Now I'm teary-eyed watching midnight stars.

Replaying the kisses to your forehead.

Wrapping my arms around your torso.

Familiar cuddling that sealed our moments.

I miss you.

My truths ache my soul.

I never was honest with us.

Truth be told, I live with this regret.

Junk Mail

I'm peeking through curtains.

Archaic delivery system has me waiting.

No Pony to Express your letters.

Return to Sender halts communications.

Open electronics sign me in.

Trapped in a matrix I look for you.

Mailbox full of hand bills.

Delete.

Delete!

DELETE!

Still no you.

I search your name.

Zero results.

You love me?

You love me not?

Searching spam folders with overflow of rhetoric.

My 4 Page Letter to you must've died with Aaliyah!

Smile

I did love you.

I prayed that someone could love you like I did.

Take your innocence and allow you to live freely.

I wanted you to smile uncontrollably and radiate your personality throughout the world.

You were magic to my land when I gave up on the spell love could cast on me.

And for that I should've done some things.

I should've checked on you when we went separate ways.

I should've looked back to see if you walked out my life fully.

When I peeked into your world, your mask told me a story.

It told my heart you were happy and free.

Little did I know you were caged around your soul.

You were locked out of your true essence.

Your heart was chained, and I think I still hold the key.

I didn't know.

I didn't know you were smiling on the outside but dying on the inside.

I didn't know the laughter were captured pictures that lasted for just that moment,

while our love lasted long after our departure.

That though others occupied your time, they underestimated your kindness.

That long after our souls mated our circus arrived back in town.

We became our own crowd!

Amazed at the acts we performed again.

High wire trapeze with new euphoric highs.

Two lovers in one car with multiple nuts piling out the vessel.

You were the ringleader.

I was happy being your main attraction.

The way we submitted to one another gave control to the giver to create great theater.

But was there pain running deep in your core?

Were you lying to your crowd of friends and crying on bedroom pillows?

Bedroom pillows soaked with my scent.

Wrapped in comforters with our activities replaying scenes in your sleep.

Was I hurting you when I thought I was loving you?

Was I hurting you though I was taking you to a place you never reached before?

Visited areas together no one else knew existed?

You were calling my name erotically, but I neglected to call your number.

I was making you question if I loved you fully.

If I cared if you were okay.

I left you on an island alone.

Just yourself surrounded by the waters I had caressed your body to release.

Fermented fluids mixed with the tears that ran because of me confusing your life.

Wonder not if I love you.

Wonder not if I'm trying to kill you softly.

Wonder not if this is a joke and if you're the fool.

Just know I do love you.

Know that I do want your happiness.

Know dreams do come true for extraordinary people like you.

Please find a smile for your face.

Find your personality that makes the sun kiss those beautiful eyes.

And if anyone asks you, tell them, you're reclaiming your time.

Reclaiming your love for self.

The Dress

She holds the dress and marvels in its beauty.
She envisioned the way it would look on her.
Pressed against her body she took herself in.
Suppressed thoughts pick a lock.
Down the dark corridor named "Forbidden/Do Not Enter", a light shines.
His voice swoons her ears.
Conversations of yesteryear ring out.
She peeks her head through the doorway.
There he was!
Staring at her with a look that would submit the strongest Queen.
"You made it" he said as he reached for her hand.
She's welcomed, crossing the threshold as energy pulls her.
Warm embraces follow as she engulfs his scent.
Soft kiss to her cheek as he whispers,
"You look amazing!"
They dance closely.
Kiss softly.
Cascade across the wood floor in unison.
She shouldn't be here.
He shouldn't be felt.
But their hearts beat on one accord.
Their souls speaks in familiar language.

"Why now?" she wonders.

"Because love never dies" he responds.

Confused that he heard her thoughts she pulls back.

He smiles and says, "Thank you for this moment."

Her eyes widen as he kisses her once again.

Her lungs inflate.

Her feet feel weightless.

Butterflies' tornado in her stomach.

She gasps for air and opens her eyes.

Staring in front of a mirror her eyes redden.

Holding the dress that marries her to another man, she sighs.

Wedded Substitutes

Nicotine to my breathless lungs.

Pulls on cigarettes to coat my wants.

Cracking fibers as the flame burns my desires.

Thoughts releasing like smoke during exhales.

Heroin to a wanting vein.

Piercing needles into skin take me away.

Rolled eyes and fluttering eyelids.

Limber corpse submitting to euphoria.

Searching for vices to mask my void.

Freedom shackled along self-worth.

Caged with imperfections and sacrifices.

Choices made that led to various addictions.

Circumvented happiness.

Buried bliss.

Abandoned admiration.

I'm free falling!

Spiraling into depression.

Neglecting my world to live in yours.

Prisoner of war instead of a disillusion dreamer.

I'm wedded to substitutes.

Mild renderings scratching the surface.

Latching to emptiness.

Peer pressuring and self-doubt

Hoping someone rescues me from myself.

But nothing changes!

Minutes become familiar.

Days Deja vu.

Years kill my psyche.

I'll try a new drug to addict my love.

A new high that can't be given.

I dislike it here.

Next lifetime is looking amazing in theses darkened clouds.

Death to my old self.

Life to who I should've always been.

Kept Place for Him

She danced with tears in her eyes.
Arms wrapped around her torso.
Hips sashay to vivid memories.
Instrumental music instrumental to them.
Walls knocking down.
Hovering object landing next to her.
He's abnormal.
Unconventional.
Mainly missed.
Slick tongue with confidence.
Deep stares that melts her midsection.
Every time he visited,
self-control with the touching.
Infraction for kissing.
Love language whispering in their moments.
He's the one that needs to leave.
Take our summer love away from her.
Take the passion.
Take the love.
Take the time.
Take the trust.
Take the moment.
Too many moments make him smile.

Too many moments make her cry.

Paragraph messages find her heart.

He feels her miles away.

She feels him,

in ways that wrestle her sheets.

Ways that pillow her thighs.

Deep sighs, she awakes to blurred vision

Laying next to another that's not him.

Moist illusions have him sleeping between them.

The man in her dream's dances.

If time was right and seasons stayed the same.

She'll board his spaceship.

Letting him explore her planet.

Counting star-filled explosions forever!

Season of…

She was in a season of leaving

I was in a season to wait it out.

Wait on messages sealed from heavens mailbox

Carried from winds gaining momentum from angel wings

Letters sealed with moisture from the rain clouds we hid from

Peeking out windows anticipating sunshine to release us

Release our fears.

Release our holds.

Release our love.

But she was in a season of leaving.

So, she left me mid conversation.

Mid kiss with panting lungs.

Mid-sentence while I was asking her to live.

Live with me forever.

Live with time strengthening our love.

Live with a love that united heaven and earth.

She left during me thanking heaven for her willing to birth from her earth.

Her season changed while my calendar read "yesterday. "

Hers read "tomorrow."

Today has me writing in the stars hoping her eyes see me.

Writing for our universe to move this retrograde.

Her leaving has me leaving my fears and adventuring with faith.

I'm searching for home.

Searching for understanding through missing love.

Searching with lights on in the daylight.

I close my eyes and see her.

I see her aura.

I feel her pulse.

I feel goosebumps from the thought of her.

I was waiting on a message that was delivered a thousand times.

A message that possessed many messengers.

Yet I closed my ears and heard your steps depart.

I know what I know now.

That I learned a million lessons.

A million lessons about wasting time.

A million lessons with empty space.

That season of leaving complied with seasons of wait; they cry from connection lost and harbored.

Connection needed to sustain.

To grant forever.

Inside happiness.

Heaven.

Earth.

And our infinite connection of love through our hourglass sand.

I have a letter written to you love; I got it approved from heaven.

Sealed it with my kiss.

The carrier is angel wings.

The content is simple.

I'm coming to be with you forever.

Visions

There are shadows,

sultrily dancing inside flickering flames.

My bedroom walls are commandeered.

All the world's a stage.

My eyes the audience.

Hyperbolic paralysis concretes me.

Egyptian cotton mummifies me.

There's beauty in the choreography.

Mesmerizing to my imagination.

The concert becomes familiar.

Fire and desire.

That connection!

My warm body with cold sweats.

The realization comes full circle.

It's passion in the fire.

Erotica in the dancing.

Myself as the lead.

A previous conquest recreated.

Disappearing in the night air.

The wick died with her love.

Love Re-Enters

Hummingbird

I search for a voice that soothes the noise.

I look over the horizon for beautiful hues.

I love through the years as days are long

Separated by space

I feel you

I hear your voice

I feel your presence

Reminiscing and foreshadowing time

I once prayed a prayer, released my heart to the winds

Submitted to the answer, crawled forward to the altar.

Interlocked hands, enthralling presence atop

Yet,

Our fingertips detached, new moments fade

I just got you back, only to wrinkle our time

Only to capsize my heart, shared breathing now fleeting

In response,

My soul has locked its corridor, angered at connection lost.

It lays in our quilted connection,

It sobs for me to accept you are Love.

The way it yells your name I hear your voice

The way it projects your aura I see your face

The way it shows your warmth, I feel your touch

My soul is waging war inside my world

Commanding for me to seek you

To confess

To never let go

To explain my thoughts

To tie my love to yours.

My soul wants you!

I want you!

I need space to shrink the distance

For timing to not be wrong

For forever and a day to be our wildest dreams,

To be wrapped in forever

To dance in the lightning

To bathe in the rain

To smile within our harvest.

I fell in love at first conversation

Loved even when love left

Within a crowded planet we find one another.

Knotted by the ribbons in the sky

I love you

I choose you

My joy and happiness

Like a southern hummingbird in concert

I'm a fan of your music!

Dear Father Time

For years if I let her down,

I vowed never to repeat the same mistakes.

Calendars turn and the simple actions still affect her.

I take mental notes to apply daily.

She's a jigsaw puzzle with the corners completed.

I'm working on her heart.

Navigating too her soul.

My prayers are to Father Time to see fit.

One more chance.

A wrinkle in time to produce hope.

My faith is in our love.

I know it runs deep.

My energy latches onto hers.

I just hope she knows I want her inner thoughts as well.

If they aren't for me then I'll fall back.

But if they are about me…

I waited my time to fully love you.

Swam an ocean with handcuffed hands.

Climbed a mountain with bound feet.

Poured my heart out during a monsoon.

Enough was always written all over you.

I poorly evaluated the time I had.

And for that I live with a regret.

One that might not grant us forever together.

So, say hello through your smile.

I'll answer with love and affection.

A broken clock is right twice a day.

I just need once more to get this right.

Idle Ideation

Idle thoughts inside ticking tocks.

The searching arm of my soul knocking on my heart's door.

Locked behind fragile emotions I question our right now.

Does she think of me while stars twinkle?

Do her alone moments hear my voice whispering in the wind?

Did she know she's my heaven?

That the angels harmonize from our love?

Knock!

Knock!

Knock!

My soul bangs a little louder.

Audible pleas that you hear my love.

Sweet sentences send signals singing serenades.

I'm drafting up the nerves to tell you my fears.

Roleplaying your responses once I confess new ways to love.

Each day the sun dances on your eyelids I'll find new ways to love you.

Each breath I hope life displays my depths.

With every blink I hope you see me in those quick dreams.

I'll bang on my heart until the confidence builds.

Thump the door until it opens and I finally tell my wants.

Please come in and make yourself at home.

My soul has been waiting on you.

My heart has fallen for you.

My mind has dreamt of you.

In moments alone I love.

Anticipation called us.

Signed letters addressed to you.

The contents forever my gratitude for loving me.

You're more beautiful than before.

More striking than lightning dancing in the night sky.

I'll be gentle with you.

Be gentle back.

We'll grow together.

Hopefully from this letter you'll write back.

I Apologize

I apologize...
For any hurt, harm, or hindrance.
Hurt I caused by being absent.
Harm I cause for not protecting you.
Hindrance for taking so long to come back.

I apologize...
For love, lust, and longevity.
Love that I gave you since day one.
Lust within our contorted frames.
Longevity cause we're still here.

I apologize...
For not kissing, hugging, or communicating.
Not kissing the lips that sparked flames.
Not hugging your heart to mine.
Not communicating I wanted more.

I apologize...
For friend zones, space, and time.
Zones you were in that you never belonged.
Space infused because of muted wants.
Time to regret the miscues and mistakes.

I apologize for looking the part.

For playing the part.

For acting the part.

For being the part.

All your needs.

All your wants

All yours!

For not completing us when you were mine!

I apologize!

Yesterday

I fantasize about a day and night.
Of presence and time.
Your heartbeat with mine.
Your touch on my skin.
Your breath as my oxygen.
I see your face inches from mine.
Solemn and peaceful.
Angelic and beautiful.

If tomorrow never had breath,
And yesterday never died.
I'll be locked in your eyes
Held in your comfort.
Shared in your space.
With trembling words and soulful sentences,
I live forever in our I love you's
Forever in the unpacked past.
Forever inside forever.
If yesterday was imagination,
then today was my indication.
That shadows have names.
Voices that belong to a soul.
I'll unearth my feelings if you lend me your ear.
Fly under water and swim in the sky

If you dwell with me forever in yesterday.

Soul Mates

Do you believe in love?

The depths of allowing someone to

intertwine their energy with yours.

The ability to morph and mold.

The understanding of release and trust.

That the touch can penetrate your soul.

That it can borrow emotions

that erupt like geysers in Yellowstone.

What if I never touched you in intimate settings?

What if you held a piece of me

that I didn't know was missing?

Why do my thoughts run back to a time

when you fluttered my dormant butterflies?

Inside lined paper you wrote.

Inside diamonds you found clarity.

Inside time we created our moment in love.

Our souls mate even with time and distance eclipsed.

Soulmates to our one.

Yet our soul mates to the love of our lives.

A Brilliant Tragedy

I smile when I think of her.
Uncontrollable admiration for her existence.
Precious time stolen to verbalize our love.
Gentle swipe of tears.
Soft kisses to her cheeks.
Stretched arms that wrap around each other's frame.
I chase her smile.
Her hidden corky!
Her inapt ways of being vulnerable around me.
I have needs to verify her happiness.
Let's call it the friend in me.
She has a way of keeping me close.
We'll call it a "healthy soul tie."

If her spirit calls, I'm coming.
If her smile fades, I'll be on my way.
My arms will cover her.
My forehead kisses will touch her mind.
My words will ease her soul.
Our promise to never let go solidifies the intensity.
We're shadows within each other life.
Ghosts in the machine we call love.
Belonging to me she doesn't.

Yet selfishly she is mine.

I am hers.

Our reasoning is not up for debate with others!

We are their authors of Love's brilliant tragedy!

Time and Space

Best way to put it...

We are two souls intertwined.

Two orbs gravitating forever in each other's presence.

Inner system's navigating in outer regions waiting to collide.

We hold a connection that dwarfs the calculation of time.

Each hold a relic of the other.

Each relic houses the energy.

The nucleus incubates the future.

The outer spheres allow us to live apart.

But we feel each other.

Her pain pierces my gut.

My hurt quakes her heart.

The term "love" envies what we have.

When together we create a custom utopia.

Why wallow in pure hypocrisy when you dwell inside eons forever?

Why cast a lot with unfertilized soil when you are the mother to my earth?

During flickering stars, I close my eyes and reach for you.

During resting moments, I feel you dream of me.

Something leads us back to each other's presence.

Maybe this lifetime we can finally have forever.

Finally write our story for those after to immortalize us in time and space.

Dreamscape

Something's not right with somebody I know.
I can feel it deep down in my spirit.
I'm having dreams about a stranger that I once knew.
They're reaching out to me during my Dreamscape,
but I can't seem to latch hold of them.
I once protected them.
I once shielded them from the pains of this world.
But they saw fit to walk alone.
Leave without any explanation,
and search for happiness in the rugged terrain.
I received verbal postcards to let me know
that they were doing well.
Spot check-ins to touch base here and there.
Send a message by others because the confidence was weak
to pick up the phone and tell me their feelings.
So, I broke all ties.
Broke forms of communication.
But over the last few days I feel you.
I feel your spirit trying to latch back on.
I feel your spirit trying to tell me something.
Where are you going?
Tell me where you are?
I know we need to talk, but I feel like you need me

more to protect you at this moment than a conversation.

What do I need to bring?

What would it take for you to leave your current situation and walk away with me?

I can't come to rescue if you're not ready to be rescued.

I can't come ready for battle if you're setting me up for failure.

We were once on the same page.

Once on the same book and on the same chapter.

No, we're not there no more.

But if you need me, I will come running like the knight in shining armor in the trilogy.

Maybe it's not you.

Maybe it's me longing for something that I know nothing about anymore.

Maybe it's me searching seeing if you are the same person or if you truly change.

Maybe it's just me with an ounce of love left for you hoping that you're okay.

Maybe I'm the controller the Dreamscape.

Maybe I'm the one that pulls the strings on this puppeteer.

They say let sleeping dogs lie.

Yet, it feels that I'm trying to awaken the dead

and have one last kiss with what should have been destiny.

I sleep a little more.

I dream a little bit.

But if you keep coming back to me,

I might have to reach out and physically touch you.

Weathered Tone

It was her tone.

The escaping sweetness that speaks of discomfort.

A hint of irritation with a mild pinch of frustration.

Something was wrong.

Though not my place to ask I accept my position.

She needed space.

Time to manage whatever was plaguing her right now.

So, I didn't pry.

I just closed my eyes and projected my spirit to let her know I'm here.

Not close in proximity but right there.

Aligned with her to combat the perils of life causing a war.

I'll be the spotter; she's a dead shot shooter.

I'll take the wheel, getaway driver to her crime if need be.

Clyde and Bonnie!

Whatever her world was doing I would be ready to make her smile.

I'll be the punching bag to the pain.

Take it out on me; I'll accept your energy.

Whether good or bad.

Evil or joyous.

I want whatever part of you that you can give.

I heard a voice that usually serenades my soul.

A voice that sounded weathered and short.

Whenever you need me just call.

I'll come running in whichever way you need me.

Just to heal your voice, getting it back to the audible the world is use too.

Full of energy and love.

A Touch of Tomorrow

When we touch, endorphins shoot off like pyrotechnics in the sky.

Constant stares into each other's faces, we share a universe in each other's eyes.

Soft features accent a personality that holds my heart.

She grips my words with her heart.

I pull her closer with each sentence.

Every action has a reaction.

And hers are tears!

Slow forming emotions, wedged in the corner of her eyes.

I'll wipe them as they fall.

My palm on her cheek.

The fingerprint of my thumb leaves imperfections.

Modest and magnificent.

Edgy and entertaining.

I'm seated next to forever love.

Carving out a moment that needs all my attention.

She grabs my hand.

Her face says a million thank you's.

But it's the one look that freezes me.

The look of staying.

Without words she is asking me to stay.

Not just right now.

Not just tomorrow.

She wants me to stay forever.

To choose this moment and create forever.

To walk away from life and construct our dreams.

Her face melts me.

Her voice quakes me.

"What do you want from me?" he asked.

"I want you to never leave!" she said.

Those were the words that broke me.

Message to a Difficult Person

Whoa!!!

What we not goin' to do is allow certain things to be transferred over.

Once you get your fresh start it's a new beginning.

It's you cleaning out the negative thoughts.

Inserting all the new positive ones in their place.

Never do you have to accept anything unless you or the relationship you're in showcase the trait that needs to be altered.

I've been standing in the gap for months.

I'm proud of the woman you have become.

You're not difficult.

Your version of love needs to be learned and appreciated.

It's pure and vicarious.

To stagnate your innocence is to kill a part of you.

If I'm the one, let me breathe life into you.

Let me kiss emotions back in your heart.

Please allow our souls to finally have each other.

I'll continue to wipe the tears away.

They'll be from you realizing that love last eons.

I'm complex and you're straightforward.

Yet, you're reserved and nurturing with me.

Well, if you will ever have me,

I'll be simplistic and caring.

Loving and giving.

Protecting and understanding.

Whatever the difficulties you are speaking of...

We'll work through them together

Just like we have done with our love.

The Photograph

Maybe I wasn't good at love.

Maybe others loved me and that was enough for them.

Maybe I masked my happiness with struggled wants.

Gave my needs limited ability to transform forever.

Maybe I second guessed our first date.

Realized my thoughts run free like unlock asylum doors.

Stared at you only when you weren't looking.

Scared to pierce your soul with eye contact.

Maybe leaning into kiss was too soon.

Maybe you turning your cheek was needed.

How far could one kiss go?

If done right...

Pass the respect factor and into the abyss.

The water's gone that you allowed me to dwell in during past years.

Open pores with open legs.

Warm bodies with vigorous heartbeats.

Completion of an activity premature for our forever.

Kissing you would've been everything.

Even the end of us before we got started.

Maybe practical isn't us.

Smiles from ear to ear as we people watch for laughter.

Conversation in our own language since communication gives us life.

Maybe I'll take in your pictures a little while longer.

Mesmerize my love through your piercing eyes.

Witness beauty in a still frame.

Classic black and white's that cement you in time.

Organic smiles which warns my soul.

Maybe you color in every form.

A chart with so many hues that only I'm able to see.

Whatever it is I'm devoted.

To be with you in each picture.

To show everyone we're finally coupled

Loves

Flames

Rekindled

The Freedom of Love

It's the small things she cherishes.

Fragments of moments building memories.

Later reflections that warm her heart.

She loved a listener.

A jotter of notes.

Mentally learning her quirks.

Successfully executing tangible surprises.

A man that flowed effortlessly with her.

A man that judged not and loved deep.

A man that passionately stimulated her throughout the day.

She uses checklists to evaluate.

He checks her boxes and ask what else.

Speechless at his commitment.

Marveled at how he knows her.

Connected like Siamese twins.

Conjoined were their souls.

Fuming flames of fire when close.

A subtle symphony of music to each other.

The distance they traveled through.

Quadrants that caused their love to run off cliffs

To soar when scared.

To fly to unknowns.

To achieve one thing.

Happiness!

Their hearts mingled with laughter.

Their souls carried their depths of love.

Their minds together were precision.

Loving each other is uncomplicated.

Belonging to one another was the complexity.

If only life gave them more than occurrences.

More than coincidental visits.

Maybe then they could sculpt a new world.

Build on foundations that hold forever.

Tell stories of a love that taught and gave.

A love that didn't take or steal.

Forever memories of a million firsts.

A million reasons a day to love each other

without boundaries.

A lock and key turned to unlock the freedom of love.

A story heaven has been waiting to tell the universe.

Simply Beautiful

She was sexual without intercourse.

Erotic and enticing with a kick of spice.

Great conversation that owned blank stares.

She controlled her wants, vaulting her needs.

Happiness and respect started the list.

A smile accents anticipation whenever I called.

Butterflies and soft words when we meet.

All the love I have is what I'm giving.

Just be good to me, and the universe is yours.

Be my earth!

I'll caress your lands.

Swim in your seas.

Forehead kisses to your "north pole."

Gentle foot massages to your "south."

Diligence at your "equator."

Simply beautiful to me.

Sunshine on windowpanes as melted bodies separate.

Long stares into each other soul.

Words tell our story.

Actions reverberate for eons.

If she's my day, I'm chasing the sun.

If she's my night, I'm tracing constellations.

Signing her name,

on her skin,

with my tongue!

I'm willing to satisfy on command.

Awaiting your approval to give you whatever you can handle.

I'll be gentle.

Just awaiting your command!

A Flickering Amber

She's the lesson of love that never left my side.

The energy that pulls my faults.

The understanding of my wants.

The completion of my needs.

Our love dances inside flicker flames.

Our memories are amber's that create a fiery passion.

Lips marry as tongues wrestle.

Fermented womb trickle nectar to the gateway entrance.

Bulging pride inches up her stomach during hugs.

Attraction energizes the mind and choreography begins.

The small of her back rest my massaging hands.

Pulled hair exposes a tasteful neck to tantalize with kisses.

Gentle placement on her back she submits.

Disappearing act with thighs earmuff his head.

Arched back with open mouth,

she can taste ecstasy in the bedroom air.

Her heaving stomach pushes freedom through her bones.

Goosebumps and questions; he took her to the summit.

Her body and mind separate.

His body and width peruse.

Uncharted quadrants of her cave seek exploration.

Shadows dance alongside bedroom walls.

Their contortionists with fluid movement.

I love you sit atop their lips.

She releases first.

He releases second.

Number two isn't so bad

when the top spot has his name engraved on it!

Last Time

Before I leave...

Kiss me like tomorrow is dying

Each ticking minute erasing tomorrow's promise.

Lay with me!

Allow me to give my all.

Accept as much as you can grasp.

You first!

Me last!

Release as much as you like.

As much as you can.

I'll be patient.

Because tomorrow might not be written.

Bottle Rockets and Boat Anchors

I asked...

Have you ever had a bottle rocket shot off in your house?

Let someone drop a boat anchor in you that will stop the Titanic?

Have you ever rolled your eyes and hips at the same time?

Lost consciousness slightly but felt your world moving?

Have you ever wanted more than what you got?

Only to realize that a second helping is far from gluttony.

Well, we can feast anyway.

Day and night.

Night and day.

Just tell me your preference.

Oh, it's whatever I want!

Well, that's simple.

Just lay there.

Try not to move.

Have you ever lost control, while in control?

If not it's about to take place.

Within this room lay your head, please arch your back.

Between your shoulder blades I'll rest my hand.

I just want to balance you out.

Take the small of your back to lift your pelvis.

Lock your legs around me.

Matter fact place your feet on my chest and let them butterfly out.

Are the moans for me?

Are your eyes usually in your thoughts?

How about you roll on your side?

Legs scissors with me in between.

That pillow won't help you.

Wait, the neighbors might hear.

Especially when my right-hand drums a beat on your backside.

The left holds the back of your neck.

I'm not responsible for you moving your hips.

The Lord wouldn't like you cursing while saying his name.

Those tremors are turning into earthquakes.

Your face is flushed.

Am I causing the teeth imprint on your bottom lip?

That wasn't my intention.

I only intended to talk to you with a mouth full of your insides.

Have you questioning why I knew that spot.

Let you release.

Then I come in.

Have you wondering why.

Only to lose your focus.

Change positions when I get close.

Have you look down and wonder where I'm going inside you.

Holding on to my trunk.

Your lips vertically massaging with each movement.

Bottle rockets and boat anchors.

Fireworks shoot off in your water.

Love Note

Good morning love!
I hope this scribe kisses your forehead
with admiration and love.
That it wraps your core like melted bodies
sleeping through the night.
Bicep pillows that rest your weary head.
Opposite arm swaddled around your frame.

Good morning love!
I wish we never left.
Never let go.
Never said bye.
Never turned and walked away.
Formulated tear in my eye.
The pain of breaking our connection.

Love, as morning wrestles you in your bed.
I'm scribing you my happiness.
I would want to be the first to tell I love you.
First look in the morning.
Last look at night.
The eliminating of wondering and guessing.
This is confirmation that time is on our side.

Good morning love!

7 Days Ago

It's been I week since, well you know.

A week since I had a hold of you.

A week since I had to let go.

7 days since you smiled at me.

Days since you laid with me.

Honest communication about my love of thee.

Foreshadowed thoughts about future life.

Ring talk about what you need as a wife.

Removed walls that let me enter your soul.

Drawn lines in the sand not to cross your outlined threshold.

No kissing with lips, ignition of fire.

Days since will power burned our desires.

Fetal position bodies melted together.

Connected as one like we had forever.

Yet time never slowed.

Never waited or was put on hold.

Just a pocket of time and space.

Deep stares mentally capturing your face.

Soft rubs on your frame.

Your roaming hands did the same.

Tornadoes and rain.

Abstaining became pain.

If only for the night.

Panting breathing and closed sight.

A few scratch marks with deep neck kisses.

Cursing and ecstasy as I fulfill your wishes.

Yet we slept the night away.

Only us to know, as the walls had no say.

My arm your pillow.

Sunshine on our morning window.

We allowed this happenstance.

7 days ago, I fell in love again at morning's first glance.

Sleepovers

It's something about the way my ocean of thoughts crash against the banks of imagination.

The way the moon squeezes creativity like lemonade hugs from lost love.

Dancing beetles with glowing bodies searching for affection in the dark sky.

Claim winds with hinting whispers serenading a soul awaiting to be touched.

Black skies with stationary stars, comets shooting across carrying passengers reconnecting with love.

Silent prayers of protection and traveling grace.

Kites flown without strings as heaven hears my wants.

Needed characteristics assemble my orchestra of fluid motions.

I'm playing poetic songs from my soul in hopes it reaches the desired residence.

Unlock doors and programmed steps navigate with the lights off.

Danity strides eliminate the creaking of my presence climbing to desired heights of reaching you.

Open the close bedroom door, we'll lock the world out.

You're the sand at the beach I'll forever bring.

The glistening glow of shimmering perfection and sculptured beauty.

Crashing waves during high times deep in the wee hours of wrestling shells and suppressed wants.

Forehead kisses with arms clutching to love like thieves in the night.

Laying on my back I hold fast to dreams.

I let go once and you disappeared like a ghost in thin air.

I watched us sunset our love.

Found it years later as the moon pierced my window one night.

Waves on the embankment of life.

Crash your love into me once more.

Stay past daybreak and daytime warmth.

Through evening sunsets and witching hour harmonies.

Your pocket watch pillow is forever home awaiting your soul to activate our chronograph.

Arm straddled between two mountain peaks,

I'll melt with you the minutes and seconds of our forever.

Crashing waves against your coastal walls that forever hangs my picture within your ocean interior.

Brown Eyes

I stare!

Mesmerized at their beauty.

Her soul speaks through them.

Her essence cries out.

She blinks away the past.

Tears of joy.

So much hidden behind pupils.

They become the gateway to her soul.

The staircase to her heart.

The benefactor of her emotional release.

Focus on our future.

See me for who I am.

Admire me for who I become.

Can you see forever with me?

A future of never ending.

A love transcending.

Through your brown eyes,

I see my destiny!

Speak To Me

Her eyes speak to me.

I hear "what if" and "maybe when."

No regrets in her tone.

Just admiration for a world that could've been.

Soft and sensual.

Brown pupils with piercing prospective.

Her heart says hello.

Her soul asks if I'm the one.

That smile.

That smile invites me into her wildest thoughts.

Years of history.

We've been studying each other subjects for decades.

Though our lips never touched,

we passionately kiss the world we could've known.

I forever look into her eyes because they key my lock.

They turn me on.

They spark a brush fire.

Only her wetness I give her can drench the land.

Submissive

His tone is defining!

Her body accepting!

His lips to her ear.

Her goosebumps on his skin.

Deep sighs to the heavens.

Full meal to his appetite.

Alpha woman to Alpha male.

Yet, agile as she waterfall.

Inside out.

Her outsides dance.

Tango and Two-Step.

She let go of her pain.

Transferring her energy.

She's submissive to his control.

Nature At Its Best

Soft kisses to skin.

Light piercings open your pod.

Taste buds process your nectar.

Receptors measures your quality.

Liqueur drips from exclusive crop.

Your fermented bottle now open.

Consumption drenches my pallet.

Sipping drop by drop.

Drunken off your nature.

Equilibrium's off!

Legs wrap around long stem.

Tension with heavy breathing.

Nature at its best.

I indulge in your essence.

I come here often!

Love Next Steps

Frozen Moment

Her lap feels like home.

My head nestles under her bosom.

My ear to her jukebox.

Erotic tones swooning my eardrums.

Warm thighs kiss my cheeks.

My closed eyes reminisce of her forever place.

She plays in my hair.

Twist and turns, she unravels my thoughts.

I roll on my back to see her face.

Heavenly!

Golden hue of her skin.

Sweetest smile of a welcoming soul.

Rest easy on my bicep.

On my side of the bed, we melt into one.

Forever yours.

I love you!

Angel Number

When you sleep,

I clutch my pen and hone my artistry.

Cursive script in the night sky.

Eyes gaze out of windows.

Body nestled into beds.

Replays of honest dialogue.

Twist and turns.

Words begin to breathe.

Sentences begin to live.

I'll write a million words.

That'll tell you a billion ways.

That I love you!

In our language.

Our story, told by connection.

Our smiles, memories we set free.

Why hold on to the past?

Our present melts our soul.

Life has us right here.

Right in this moment of forever.

When you sleep, I write you love letters in the night sky.

Even if daybreak comes, they still kiss your forehead with affection.

Because the message is simple.

"Thank You Lord for My Human!"

(As the angels rejoice)

Sincerely,

1111

Admiration

It was soft eyes rooted in admiration.

I walked my sight around her curves.

I raced my thoughts as I envisioned her in my world.

Sun kisses on her skin dust a golden hue.

Waves within her hair blow through the breeze.

My fandom was private.

Her aura was contagious.

Time.

Space.

Want.

I needed to just say hello.

Infatuation bits my lip.

Curiosity carves a smile.

I fell for something special.

I love(d) someone amazing.

Her kisses still linger on my lips.

Her aroma effervescent like the first encounter.

Sealed memories dance within a fragile labeled box.

Silhouettes of our shadows tell stories inside intimate confines.

Before there was ever a doubt, there was an absolute attraction.

And before I ever say goodbye, I passionately say I love you.

In her game of life, I play my position.

Forever ready to be an option.

Forever loving that we both seem to want forever together.

If forever is promised, then I promise to stay her biggest admirer.

Are You Complicated to Love?

I'm admitting that loving me is easy.
I will need love reciprocated at times.
I will need to invade your personal space
on my rough days to be held.
I will need open dialogue
and the ability to create communication
via written words.
I need to be able to provide
and always work hand and hand as one.
I need someone to make love to me
because they love to please me.
I need them to allow me to let them release first,
then when I feel like you can't take anymore,
together
simultaneously
we erupt.
I need them to understand my ever-evolving mind
to the best of their ability.
I need them to teach me the things I need to learn of them to eliminate assumption.
I need them to stay true to themselves
and never second guess whether our love is real.
And I need them to understand that other factors of loving me
and them might come about...

I just need them to grow and evolve together as one.

Reassurance

Thank you for accepting me.

There are things I never understood that you did.

Maybe this will put a lot into prospective.

You never tried to change me.

Never pushed an agenda to rearrange me.

You gave time and space the opportunity to do it for me.

I don't know if you wanted it that way or it just happened.

Just know you are the only person that let maturity manifest in me.

You accepted me and my faults.

Loved me unconditionally, even when loving me needed allotment.

You are the quintessential reason for my unconditional love for you.

If you need reassurance look no further than yourself.

You've been my biggest supporter and best friend through the years.

You gave me life multiple times and didn't know it.

So, my reasons for loving you are the same traits of yours you wonder about.

Stay true to yourself.

I'll always stay true to you.

Loving all of you until my last breath.

Dancing Sunshine

I wake up with dancing sunshine upon my skin.
A sweet smile on my heart.
Warm admiration in my soul.
A stain moment in my mind.
I wake up to a Sunday moment.
A wrinkle in time that moves my body.
A moment in life that tops my memories.
The knowledge of understanding.
We blanket each other!
I wake up inside a still frame.
Holding a body that fits my core.
Head on my biceps, I pillow her pain.
Back to chest, I don't want to let go.
We hold on till time says, "it's time."
I wake up feeling your heartbeat!
Thumping on my left palm I still feel you.
All of you!
Every ounce you awarded me with.
I still feel you!
The soft tone of your voice.
I still hear you!
I love your eternal scent that coat my lungs.
Deep breaths of your essence blooms inside of me.

Warm skin touch as receptors ignite.

You're the fire to my blaze.

The water to my thirst.

I wake up holding on to my memories.

Holding on to my one day soon.

Each morning I wake up holding on to you.

I wake up holding a missing piece to a jigsaw puzzle.

The puzzle that is a completed picture of "Us!"

Dreams and Nightmares

If I face my fears, then the outcome is uncertain.
Choreography steps that now walk in faith.
Belief in self that now finally finds freedom.
Jagged blades against old wounds I cut.
Slow separation with unearthed questions.
Pulled back layers awaiting answers to finally showcase clarity.
Reality now stops, as the present looks weird.
Jumbled colors with an array of lights.
Fireworks on calm days.
Joyous screams inside the night air.
Vulnerability of a soft soul.
The want of kisses upon soft lips.
The loosened knot of a soul tie.
The combined fire of twin flames.
Journey with me through life.
Take my hand and trust in me.
No more standing on the cliff of life.
Decisions need to be made that will last a lifetime.
A person's fear clouds their atmosphere and drenches them with rain.
You've been my umbrella to shield me.
Now allow me to be the vessel that soars through our doubt.

Venture past our old limits.

Position the future with today's present.

Push past the overcast.

Sunset with me as we witness the horizon
change into vibrant colors.

Be my first last and my last first
to everything moving forward.

Build Me Up

Why do you know me?
My inside thoughts surrounded by outside walls.
My movements that keep me stagnate.
You're progression with just your presence.
I'm questioning everything!
Did I miss the answers to questions asked?
I'm entrenched in your essence.
Technically I'm drunken in love.
High on your scent.
I inhale your bloom.
And you allow me.
Grant me permission to protect your emotion.
To guard your body and hold your shell.
Speak volume to your core,
and wipe doubt from your mind.
And you see through me.
Pass my faults and over my dispositions.
Around my confidence to land on my heart.
You smash the bricks that build the wall.
Remove the rubbish and kiss my core.
You become my architect.
Grabbing the stone so many refused to use.
You're turning me into artwork.

Priceless and unique.

A bold story behind the inspiration.

And that inspiration is you.

You're the diligent work to display that you are enough.

Past and present.

Future and forever.

Forever trust and respect.

Always honesty with integrity.

We examined each other for years.

Happiness will be our test of time.

Pieces of Love

Marvelous Curves

Gentle hands hover over

Hourglass symmetry pleasant to the eye.

Undergarments hug peaks in the front.

Arches in the back.

Treasures of the grail.

Marvelous curves.

Perfection.

Kudos to the Sculptor.

Sincerely,

A fan of your work!

Unimpressed

Eyes fixate on their frame.

There's beauty within the sight of this beholder.

Arousal and readiness knocking inside the bedroom door.

Sweet undertones of previous talks warranted this opportunity.

I'm ready!

Ready to give!

Ready to take!

Ready to receive this moment and its mystical glory.

Then…

Soft kisses feel sloppy and untamed.

Futile attempts to enter the watery cave dock against forbidden entryways.

Frowned faces with discomfort adorn her face.

Heavy breathing like exhaustion runs through his veins.

Rolled eyes and desert sands produce uncomfortable positions.

Horizontal kisses scratch scared pearls.

Aggressive wordplay asks if it's his.

Sarcastic answers make sure he knows it isn't.

He came.

She left.

He thought he conquered.

She exited defeated and deflated.

Distanced Traveled

Last night I searched for you,
Through dreams and scenes.
I cut through midnight's air surveillance for a glimpse.
I covered terrain like a rescue party.
Getting to you was all I needed.
You could've been anywhere.
Your dreamscape could be eliminating passage.
Yet my spirit locked in on a GPS signal,
It had to be you.
Bright lights from a loving heart shined in my direction.
Outstretched arms with smiling face warmed the embrace.
Your soft tone in my ear saying your happy I made it.
Away from the world, I found you in my dreams.
Our bodies apart in distance, yet our spirits connected.
Energy and love.
Twins from the same flame.
Last night I found you within my dreams.
This morning I close my eyes and wonder
if you can feel my forehead kiss.

If Lips Kissed

I didn't understand at first why our lips couldn't meet.

Elongated moments of affection trapped within passion.

Fibers pulsating forever as endorphins rushed.

Her lips were the pillows that slept my soul.

The soft knocks on my heart's door that unlocked for only her.

Fluent tongue wrestlers communicating wants.

I thought the need was to show her I still loved her.

To kiss her back into my life.

We were missing pieces to a jigsaw that involved one another.

Travelers on one road in separate directions that collided in ecstasy.

I tried to lean in and mouth my affection.

She leaned back and cancelled the action.

Something so simple would bring complexity into our lives.

Something so blissful could irrigate deserts and flood sands.

She always looked like everything!

The emergence of wants.

The resurrection of needs.

If horizontal lips kissed, then friendship would be the rearview.

So, I softly touched her skin.

Letting my fingers climb her goosebumps.

I'm walking around them speaking braille.

Deep breathing like she's never been touched before.

We got time to engage in taboo things when our clocks align.

For now, I'll caress her differently.

Scribe heartfelt messages into her soul.

Showcase my wants in her dreams.

Unify my heartbeat with hers.

Until time gives me all of her,

I'll appreciate the moments that lead us into one embrace.

Staring into each other's gaze that won't ever have us looking back again.

Heart to Heart

Scattered frequency on rainy days.

I miss her vessel.

That warm body that locks into mine.

Those kisses that lead

Lead us into a new galaxy

Exploding stars in the distance.

Wherever we are I'll be yours.

My heartbeat thumps with yours.

Your breath inhales my lungs.

We've been loving each other since first touch.

Twisted souls knotted.

Keyed and locked together.

She never worried about distance,

I was hers because our souls spoke.

Forever hers.

My Mother Earth imported from Venus.

I was her Mars trying to close the gap.

Longing for her again.

I'll roll the dice and bet, she's all I need.

Fly a spaceship to her center.

Love on her until our sun sets.

Caress time as we walk the sands of her hourglass.

Wherever she resides we'll build in her city.

Foundation of love.

Walls built with trust.

A cathedral roof of faith.

I'll sail her oceans,

Bathe in her waters.

Same frequency each day of our life.

Soothing music that sings our connection.

Slow dancing under moonlight.

The world is ours,

No space or time to interrupt.

Forever kisses to worthy lips.

Pen Pals

We are pen pals,

scribing flirtatious sentences that kisses the soul.

Custom keys to each other's lock.

A specific interval within the hourglass.

No need to bring sand, she's the beach.

I'm the waves that pressed against her shore.

High tide!

Low tide!

Calming movements under God's sky.

We bleed our ink.

Masqueraded emotions of the past unmask the truth we never told.

The canvas we write on tells a story that never ended.

The bee and the lotus flower.

The pollination that dances on her pedals.

She blankets me. Holds me close without touch.

Shields me when it rains with no umbrella.

Yet I should've been the soil that planted her.

Put her in my soil to grow around and through me.

My pen pal tells me their wants.

Outlines her needs.

Replays our past.

Unpacks the miscues.

Talks for understanding.

And after delivery we both drift!

Back to reality.

Back a world without each other's presence.

I'll write you more often, just write me back.

I'll sign it "I love you" because I truly do.

Holding my breath under water until you give me breath again for life.

Mercury Retrograde

There were illusions in my orbit.

Reverse direction as my past speaks to my future.

There lies the problem.

Random activity from frequent people irrelevant to my right now.

Yet, they shoot air balls at rimless goals.

Frozen phones and dropped signals.

Glitching TVs with nothing to watch.

Held space in solitude my phone finally rings.

Unlikely but always on time.

An old misunderstanding that understands my miscues.

So much history written between us.

A tragic love story with epic connection.

Mercury is spinning backwards.

Now my thoughts are as well.

Reminiscing on the past with old love.

Oh, how stars coated night skies as we wrestled like grown-ups.

A celestial event with clouds of love resting our frames.

She was my earth, allowing my planet to pass through her life quickly.

Then I was gone.

Distance and measures between us with a connection that never left.

Energy harnessed for future usage.

A date for reconciliation once our planets is in eyesight.

On a line within a document, I'll sign my name.

Forbidden fruit bearing seeds to plant within her soil.

Barren lands kissed by my lips allows for irrigation

Living water to flow through deserted canals.

Years add up as we subtract the distance.

I'm closer to forever with you.

Echoing all the "never" occurrences that whisper our love.

To Whom It Does Concerns,

It's the radio silent communication strangling my emotions. Empty receiver out of order as I replay your voice. I'm flipping through pictures drowning in your absence. I've penned you a letter that must not haven't gotten to you. I unlocked my soul with the key you returned. The way it cried poetically created a collection of honesty.

I've been lost without you. Searching for our twinkling star in the night sky hoping you are wondering about me. I type messages that ask to see your face. I delete the sentence and never send my wants.

You are my crippling agent that swirls my psyche if told no.

So, I speak not.

Not to you.

Not through messages.

Not by calls.

I whisper in the winds and hope that it blows your way.

I regret so much.

I miss all of you.

The embrace of hugging as we melted for moments. The soft pillowed lips igniting endorphins. Your voice of reasoning and wisdom throughout conversations. My head on your lap as your fingers dance in my hair. The way our bodies intertwine we squeezed the fruitful nectar of passion.

You are everything to my dreams.

The lost wants that found a need.

The guarantee that a love like this last forever.

Clocks tell time as time tells truth. Through the years I never stopped loving you, I only walked away to let you grow. Scribbling inside this letter I realize we've walked away again. Well, if our tomorrow isn't promised. If the present has given up. I believe the universe grants fate. Still gives life and doesn't take love away from the future.

I give you, my love.

My love inside these words.

Inside the margins of life.

I'm writing poetry hoping it finds your heart. That heart that I want combined as one with mine. I'll search the universe. Leave letters at all your listed addresses. Read aloud my renderings. All for the hope that you still believe in creating a masterpiece that will be told for eons.

It's outside my power.

My soul has penned.

My eyes have cried.

My emotions depleted.

Kisses don't last forever, but a love like ours lives forever.

Forever yours,

Your Twin Flame

About the Author

KEFENTSE BOOTH

Like a classic Picasso painting, his literary genius doesn't just leap off the pages—it gets into the heart and soul of the reader. Mirroring the style and prose of literary greats such as Robert Frost, Langston Hughes and Maya Angelou, Kefentse Booth not only paints vivid pictures with his choice of words—he immerses the reader so deep into the situation at hand that they hardly ever have time to come up for fresh air.

In his current works, Miles Traveled Down Love's Highway and Stranded on Love's Highway, Booth takes readers on a journey of life lessons and the reality of relationships. No matter where readers choose to get on this sensual highway, they will experience pain, pleasure, and fiery passion—even if they only read one excerpt. Written from a personal perspective of his past mishaps, mistakes and misfits, Booth strives to intertwine the realistic, yet unexpected love life of the average reader—allowing readers worldwide to not only see themselves but feel themselves in the moment. Because of his great love for all things literary, Booth founded Street Light Dreams, LLC, where he cultivates and educates writers to pursue their passion and become published authors.

CPSIA information can be obtained
at www.ICGtesting.com
Printed in the USA
LVHW100913261022
731518LV00003B/59